THE FRIENDLY ROBIN

Billy and Susan watched the birds that
came to eat from their bird table
and their special favourite was a robin.
In the spring, just when they
thought they could watch the robin
build a nest the two children caught
measles and had to stay in bed.
But the friendly robin had a
pleasant surprise for them.

Enid Blyton

The friendly robin

Illustrated by Constance Marshall

KNIGHT BOOKS

the paperback division of Brockhampton Press

ISBN 0 340 18741 7

This edition published 1974 by Knight,
the paperback division of Brockhampton Press, Leicester.

These stories first published in Stories and Notes
to Enid Blyton Nature Plates 1949 by Macmillan and Co.
Copyright. All rights reserved.
Illustrations copyright © 1974 Brockhampton Press Ltd.
Printed and bound in Great Britain
by
Cox & Wyman Ltd., London, Reading and Fakenham

*Nine stories
about animals, birds,
fish and plants*

Contents

The friendly robin

Billy and Susan had a bird-table. They put food on it in the winter, and many birds came to eat it. The one they liked the best was the little red robin.

'He's so friendly,' said Billy. 'He sits on the edge of the table, and puts his head on one side and looks at us as if he really liked us.'

'I love his rich little song,' said Susan.

Sometimes the robin flew to the window-sill and looked in at the window, as if to say, 'Hurry up and put the food out! I'm hungry!' Once he even pecked at the window.

When the spring came, the birds found plenty of food in the bushes, hedges and ditches, and they did not need the bird-table any more.

Billy and Susan saw the robin sometimes, and he sang to them. They wondered where he would build his nest.

'We'll go and look for it soon,' said Billy. 'He hasn't built it yet, because he hasn't chosen a wife.'

But before they could go and look for it, both children got measles! They had to go to bed, and they were very sad about it.

'Just as the nice days are coming!' said Billy. 'It really is bad luck!'

The children were not allowed to read because their eyes were rather bad. They grew tired of playing with their toys in bed. Mother was busy and could not read to them very much.

'I'm bored,' said Susan, and she began to cry. 'I want to go out of doors. I'm tired of being in bed.'

'Look! There's the robin come to see us!' said Billy suddenly. On the window-sill stood their little red robin. His red breast glowed brightly and his big black eyes looked at both children in surprise.

He had missed them in the garden. He had

come to look for his little friends. The window was open at the top, and the robin flew in. He sat on the end of Billy's bed-rail and sang a few notes.

Then he went to Susan's bed-rail and sang to her too.

'You darling!' said Susan, pleased. 'Oh, it is lovely to see you again! Come every day, please.'

The robin flew round the room, and looked at everything. He saw himself in the mirror and sang very fiercely, for he quite thought it was another robin there. Then he flew out.

Next day he was back again, and this time he stayed quite a long time. The children were full of delight. They lay and watched him flit round the room. He flew to the top of the cupboard and stayed there quite a long time.

Then he sang a little song and flew out of the window.

Next day—what a surprise! He was back again—but this time he brought another robin with him. She was very like him, and her red breast shone brightly. She was not at all shy, and sang a little song from the top of the mirror. Then the cock-robin took her to the top of the cupboard.

'Susan!' said Billy in excitement. 'I believe—I do believe—that the robins are going to build their nest on the top of the cupboard!'

He was right. They began to build that very day. They flew in with all kinds of things in their beaks! Sometimes they brought bits of grass and sometimes they brought dead leaves.

'They must have brought scores of dead leaves!' said Susan, with a laugh. 'Billy, don't let's tell anyone about our robins. Do let's keep it a secret—our very own secret.'

'Well, it's really the robins' secret,' said Billy. 'So we couldn't possibly give it away. Oh, Susan—isn't it fun lying here and watching the two robins fly in and out with their leaves and grass and moss?'

Mother was pleased to see the two children looking so happy. When the robins heard anyone coming to the room, they flew out quickly, so nobody but the children saw them.

The nest was soon built. The children got out of bed, climbed on a chair and saw it. It was a big nest. The robins had lined it with hairs and some little feathers. Susan put her hand inside. It was very soft and warm.

'The hen-robin got into the nest and worked herself round and round in it to make it that pretty cup-shape,' said Billy. 'I saw her. She didn't mind me looking at her at all. She's pretty, with her big black eyes and her bright red breast.'

Soon the children were well enough to get up and go downstairs. They hoped that no one would discover the robins.

'They have laid five eggs now,' said Susan one day. 'I stood on a chair and looked. Five eggs!'

'What are they like?' asked Billy.

'They are white, speckled with light red,' said Susan. 'They are very pretty. Stand on a chair and look at them, Billy.'

Billy did. The hen-robin was sitting on her nest. She must have known that Billy wanted to see her eggs, because she flew off, and he saw the five pretty eggs. She flew back to her nest again, and settled down on the eggs to keep them warm. She was very proud of them.

The cock-robin brought all kinds of food to his mate. He brought worms, grubs, flies and spiders, and the hen-robin opened her mouth,

quivered her wings prettily, and ate them all.

Then one day the eggs hatched out! What an excitement there was, for the children were just as pleased as the robins! There was a child standing on a chair peeping at the top of the cupboard nearly every hour of the day!

'Whatever do you keep running up to your bedroom so often for?' asked Mother in surprise.

The baby robins soon grew. They were very sweet. They had no red breasts, but their chests were speckled instead.

'I suppose red would be too dangerous a colour to give to young birds who don't know how to look after themselves,' said Susan wisely.

The two robins had a very busy time feeding their young ones. The five babies were always hungry, and as soon as they heard one of their parents coming, they would shoot up in the nest, open their brightly coloured mouths, and wait for a packet of food to be dropped inside.

'I suppose when one is fully fed, he doesn't pop his head up for a time, and the others get a turn,' said Susan. 'How busy the big robins are, aren't they?'

Then the children had a shock.

'I am going to have your bedroom spring-cleaned tomorrow,' said Mother. 'There seem to be a lot of dead leaves and bits of moss there—I can't think where it all comes from.'

'Oh!' said Billy and Susan in dismay. Now their secret would be found out, and perhaps the birds would be turned out of the bedroom. That would be dreadful.

But that very day the old robins thought that it was time for the young ones to learn to fly. So, much to the children's delight, they saw the babies trying to flutter round their bedroom.

It was surprising how soon they learnt to use their wings. Then out of the window they went, one after another, into the sunny garden.

'Now they will learn to fly properly, to feed themselves, and to look out for danger,' said Billy. 'Well, we *have* had fun, Susan, watching our robin family grow up, haven't we? We *are* lucky!'

Mother was most astonished when she found the robins' nest on the cupboard. She laughed when the children told her all about it.

'You should have told me before, and let me share such a lovely secret,' she said.

The squirrel who forgot

There was once a squirrel who had a very bad memory.

'You haven't a memory at all,' said Bobtail the rabbit. 'You have a forgettery.'

'I know,' said poor Bushy the squirrel. 'I do try to remember things. But I always seem to forget.'

He was a very pretty creature. He was red-brown, and his tail was very thick and long and bushy. He looked at Bobtail out of large black eyes, and listened to him with long pointed ears.

Bushy had forgotten where his resting-place was. He had built himself such a nice one in a tree. Bobtail had watched him.

Bushy had taken twigs to make it, and strips of thin bark that he had pulled from trees. He had made it cosy with moss and leaves. It was his own home, his own resting-place, where he could sleep if he wanted to.

And now he had forgotten where he had built it! Bobtail had met him whilst he was looking.

'I can tell you where it is,' said Bobtail. 'It's in a tree not far from my cousin's burrow. I'll take you.'

So he ran to a big tree not far off. Bushy bounded from bough to bough above, following Bobtail. He gave a tiny bark of delight.

'Yes—it's here! Oh, thank you, Bobtail. I really will try to remember things in future.'

The summer went by. Bushy had a lovely time. He scampered up and down trees, his big claws helping him to hold on tightly. He played with the other red squirrels. He talked to the rabbits and the birds. He didn't forget where his resting-place was, and he liked curling up there when he was tired.

Autumn came. The nights were cold, and Bushy took some more moss into his home. He didn't like the wind blowing into cracks, so he stuffed them up. It was very clever of him.

Bobtail spoke to him one day. 'Bushy, the winter is coming soon. Are you going to sleep the cold days away? The frog does, and the snake, and so does the toad. Will you?'

'I think I will sleep when it is very, very cold,' said Bushy. 'But I don't want to miss any warm sunny weather. I think the frogs and snakes are silly not to wake up as soon as a warm spell comes.'

'So do I,' said Bobtail. 'I am awake all the winter, you know, Bushy. I don't like sleeping the time away. Sometimes it is hard for me to get food if the snow is on the ground. I suppose you will not want any food if you sleep most of the time?'

'Oh yes, I shall,' said Bushy at once. 'I shall be very hungry when I wake up, if the sun comes out in the middle of winter. I must have some food then.'

'But there won't be any,' said Bobtail. 'What will you do?'

'I shall store some up for myself,' said Bushy. 'Squirrels always do that, you know. We are clever at that.'

'What will you store away?' asked Bobtail.

'Watch me and see,' said Bushy, and he began to get very busy. His food was the seeds out of pine-cones, the nuts from the hazel trees, the beech-mast from the beech trees, and things like that.

He took many hazel nuts, which were now ripe and had fallen to the ground. He hid them in a hole in the hollow tree. He found plenty of

beech-mast, and he hid that in a hole in a bank. It was fun.

'I shall have plenty of food when I wake up,' he told Bobtail. 'More than enough! Look, I am putting a heap of nuts under this stone.'

'I hope you will remember where you are putting everything,' said Bobtail. 'You know what a funny sort of memory you have.'

'Of course I shall remember,' said Bushy.

That night the first hard frost came. How cold it was! Bushy curled himself up in his tail, and slept soundly in his big nest. He did not wake the next day. It was too cold for squirrels to wake! Rabbits were about, and hares, but not a squirrel was to be seen!

The frost grew bitter. Bushy slept even more soundly. His tail kept him warm. He was cosy and snug in his moss-lined nest.

And then the frost went away, and the rain came. After that the sun came out and put warm fingers on Bushy's nest. It was not spring. It was the middle of winter, but still, for a few days, it would be quite warm.

Bushy woke up. He put his nose out of his resting-place, and his big tufted ears listened. It was a nice day. The sun was beautiful in the bare wood.

'I am hungry,' said Bushy. 'I shall go to find the food I hid away. There will be plenty.'

Off he went, scampering and bounding lightly down the tree, into the next one, across the branches, and then down the trunk to the ground.

He began to hunt for the nuts he had hidden away. But he couldn't remember where he had put them! It was no good, he just—couldn't— remember!

He sat in the wood and scratched himself just behind his tufted ears. 'Where did I put those nuts? I do want to get my sharp teeth into the shell, and gnaw a hole, and get at the sweet kernel inside. I am so hungry.'

He gritted his teeth together, wishing he had a nut to gnaw. He set off again, hunting here, there and everywhere. But not one hiding-place could he remember.

Bobtail didn't come, or he could have asked him. It was very sad. Bushy had never been so hungry in all his life.

And then he saw another red squirrel. He

didn't know this squirrel. She came bounding
up a tree, looking very frightened.

'A woodman has cut down the tree in which
I had my home,' she said to Bushy. 'I am afraid.
I have no nest now, nowhere to sleep on a cold
night.'

'And I have no food,' said Bushy sadly. 'I
have forgotten where I put my nuts and my
beech-mast.'

23

'I know where I put mine,' said Frisky, for that was her name. 'Come, and I will show you. There is enough for us both.'

Frisky had a good memory. She remembered where her stored-up food was, and soon she and Bushy were sharing it hungrily.

'Thank you very much,' said Bushy. 'That was lovely. I really did feel very hungry. Now, would you like to share my resting-place with me? I think there is room. We could curl up together, wrap our tails round each other, and keep nice and warm.'

'Oh, thank you!' said little red Frisky, her big black eyes shining. 'I was wondering where I could sleep tonight. Are you sure there is room?'

There was plenty of room. The two red squirrels curled up together in Bushy's nest, wrapped their big warm tails round each other, and fell fast asleep. It was nice to be together. It was nice to know that there was plenty of food waiting, if they woke up, and that Frisky knew exactly where it was.

In the spring the two squirrels talked lovingly together. 'Let us make a great big nest and have some squirrel babies of our own.'

Bushy was delighted. The two squirrels found a big hole in a tree, and they built their large nest there. 'The hole is our door,' said Frisky, peeping out.

In the summer-time Frisky had three little babies. They were blind at first, and had no pretty fur, but they soon grew, opened their eyes, and grew pretty furry coats.

Frisky and Bushy were very proud of them. 'Now we are a lovely little family,' said Frisky. 'Oh, Bushy, what a good thing my tree was cut down last winter, and I came along and met you!'

'And what a good thing I forgot where my nuts were, and you gave me yours,' said Bushy. 'It was a good thing I had a bad memory that day!'

'Helping one another and loving one another are the nicest things in the world,' said Frisky, cuddling down into her cosy nest with the furry babies.

And she was quite right, wasn't she?

The two little friends

A family of ducklings were swimming with their mother duck, and she was quacking to tell them to be sure and keep close to her.

'Quack! Quack! Beware of enemies! Keep by me and I can look after you. Quack! Quack!'

She had nine little ducklings, and they were all quite used to the water now. One of them, little Webtoes, did not like keeping close to his mother.

'Mother goes so fast!' he said. 'I want to swim

into all those exciting little patches of water, and see what I can find.'

'Quack! Quack! Come along, Webby!' called his mother. 'Dear me, now where has that child gone?'

'Webby, come along!' cried his brothers and sisters. Webby paddled along after his family, and off they all went again.

But as soon as he could, Webby slipped behind again. He saw that the stream ran off a little way, making a kind of back-water. It looked so exciting.

'I really must see what is in there,' said Webby, and he swam busily away from his family. He saw a big dragon-fly sitting on a water-plant and he snapped at it. It rose into the air with such a whirr that Webby was quite frightened.

Then he felt sure he saw a frog swimming below him. Webby knew that frogs made a good dinner, so down he dived into the water, to see if he could catch the frog. His little tail stuck up into the air, and that was all there was to be seen of him.

But just below Webby there were some water-weeds growing, and Webby's neck got caught in them. He tried to free himself, but he could not. He was held fast.

'Mother! Mother!' he cried, but he was under water, and his quacks sounded like gurgles. His mother was far away and could not hear him.

Webby might easily have been drowned if someone had not come swimming busily by. It was a baby moor-hen, a little dark bird, not much bigger than Webby himself.

The baby moor-hen was most astonished to see Webby's tail sticking straight up into the air. He was even more astonished to hear the queer gurgles coming up from the water.

The little moor-hen was called Bobbin, because he bobbed his head in and out, to and fro, as he swam. He hurried up beside Webby and had a good look at him.

'What are you doing?' he asked. 'Is there anything good down there!'

'Gurgle, gurgle, gurgle,' said poor Webby, trying his hardest to get out of the weed.

'What did you say?' asked Bobbin. But Webby could answer nothing but 'gurgle, gurgle'.

28

Bobbin felt rather alarmed. He was a good diver himself, and he dived in beside Webby to see what was happening.

'Oh, you are caught in the weeds!' he cried. 'I will help you.'

He began to peck at the long weeds with his sharp little beak. He struck at them with his feet. Soon he had set poor Webby free, and the little duckling rose to the surface choking for breath.

'Oh! Oh!' gasped Webby, taking in deep breaths of air. 'I was nearly drowned. Where's my mother, where's my mother?'

His mother was far away. Bobbin was sorry for the little duckling. 'I heard a family of ducks go by a long time ago,' he said. 'You had better come with me. My mother will look after you.'

So the little black moor-hen and the yellow duckling swam side by side down the stream until they came to another little family.

This time it was a family of moor-hens—but the mother was not with them. There were six babies counting little Bobbin, and they were all exactly alike. They crowded round Webby in excitement.

'What are you? A duckling? Oh, we have never seen a duckling so close before! What a funny beak you have!'

'It isn't funny,' said Webby. 'It's just the right shape for shovelling round in the mud of the pond. I find plenty of water-insects down in the mud. It's a good beak for that sort of thing.'

'Our beaks will be red when we grow up,' said the little moor-hens, 'and we shall wear red garters too.'

'Where is your mother?' asked Webby, who felt as if he wanted some sort of mother there to comfort him. A big red beak looked over the edge of a kind of platform made of rushes and reeds near by.

'I'm their mother,' said a voice. 'I can't come down because I'm sitting on eggs, and they may hatch at any moment.'

Webby was surprised. 'But you've got one family already,' he said, looking round at the little moor-hens.

'I know,' said the moor-hen, 'but I like two or three families. My first lot are very good children. They will help me to feed the second lot of babies when they hatch. Come along up here and let me look at you.'

'I can't climb up,' said Webby.

'Climb like this, using the tips of your wings,' said Bobbin, and he went up the side of the big nest easily, using his feet and wings. Webby saw that he had a kind of claw on his wings to help him up. He wished he had too.

The moor-hens pushed him up into the nest. He was very glad to be there, because the mother moor-hen was kind to him and let him nestle up close to her.

'So you got caught in the weeds, did you?' she

said. 'Poor little baby. Stay with me for a while and have a rest.'

There were a lot of spotted eggs in the nest. They were not very comfortable to lie on, but they were warm. Webby told the mother moor-hen all about his adventure.

'You shouldn't have left your mother's side,' she said. 'Bobbin will take you back to her later on.'

Bobbin climbed up into the nest beside Webby. He liked the duckling very much.

'What funny feet you have!' he said to Webby,

when he saw the webs of skins between each of the duckling's toes. 'Mother, hasn't he got funny feet?'

'Well, they are very good feet for swimming, you know,' said his mother. 'Very good indeed. The webs of skin push the water away well when Webby swims, and he gets along very quickly. All ducks have webbed feet.'

'Why haven't we?' asked Bobbin, looking at his own feet. 'I want webbed feet, Mother. It would be much easier to swim if I had webbed feet. Why don't I have them? I am a swimming bird, and I think I ought to have them.'

'Yes, but you are also a walking bird,' said his mother. 'You need to walk and run, very often, and then webbed feet would be of no use to you. Sometimes you will have to run over water-weeds, and over the flat leaves of the water-lilies, Bobbin, as well as over land in the winter-time, when the ponds are frozen. You will find your clawed feet are very useful to you then.'

'Bobbin has feet rather like the hens in our farmyard,' said Webby. 'They are not a bit like the feet of a water-bird.'

'Hark! My eggs are hatching!' said the big

moor-hen suddenly. And then, to Webby's delight, he saw the shells of the eggs breaking, and out of them came another little family of moor-hens, one after another!

'I am afraid you will have to get out of the nest now,' said the big moor-hen. 'There will not be room for you, Webby. But now that my eggs are hatched, I will leave them for a while, and take you to your mother. Bobbin shall come too.'

'We'll all come!' said the tiny moor-hens. But the big moor-hen wanted them to watch over the nest for her. 'The tiny birds will not be hungry yet, so do not feed them,' she said. 'I will cover them with rushes when I leave. You must watch out for the rat for me.'

Then she and Bobbin and Webby set off to find Webby's mother. They swam merrily along down the stream, and Webby kept very close to the mother moor-hen! He didn't want to be lost again.

Suddenly the big moor-hen heard a dog barking. 'Get under the water!' she cried. 'Swim under the water!'

Then, to Webby's astonishment, the big black

bird dived under the water, and swam to the opposite bank, only her red beak showing above the surface! Bobbin did it too. It was very clever. Webby did his best, but he was very much afraid of getting caught in water-weeds again.

At last they all met the duck family coming down the stream again to look for Webby. How pleased they were to see him!

'Mother! Mother! This is Bobbin, who saved me from drowning in the water-weeds!' said Webby, swimming up to his big white mother. She gave him a gentle peck.

'Naughty duckling! Why didn't you keep close to me as I told you to?'

'Can he be my friend?' asked Bobbin. 'I want to come and see him sometimes, and I want him to come and see *me*.'

'Bobbin is a most sensible bird,' said his mother. 'You can safely let Webby be his friend.'

So Webby and Bobbin became friends, and very often you can see Bobbin swimming with the little duck family, and Webby swimming with the moor-hens.

Betty and the lambs' tails

All the children liked nature lessons. It was fun to hear about the animals and birds and flowers. They liked hunting for things in the hedges and trees, in the fields and woods.

Miss Wills, the teacher, had made a big nature chart, which she put on the wall. There was a space left for every day.

'Now,' she said, 'I want *someone* to fill in every space!'

'How can we?' asked Jack.

'Well,' said Miss Wills, 'any boy or girl who finds something new or strange or lovely in their walks, can draw it or write a piece about it in the space for that day. And they must put their name in the space too, so that we shall know who gave us that nice piece of nature news.'

'That's a fine idea,' said Betty. 'It will be fun to fill up the spaces, Miss Wills. I hope I get my name there heaps of times.'

'Well, you will have to use your eyes a little more than you do, Betty, if you want your name on the chart,' said Miss Wills. 'You are not very good at noticing things yet!'

'I shall try,' said Betty.

'I know one thing we can look for now, before the leaves grow on the trees,' said Joan. 'We can look for old birds' nests. We shan't be able to find them easily when the trees begin to leaf.'

'And we can look for new flowers, and listen to the birds beginning to sing their spring songs,' said Pat.

It was Pat who filled up the first space on the chart. He found a yellow coltsfoot, a *very* early one! He proudly drew it on the chart, and then signed his name.

Ellen filled the next space. She saw a lark fly up from the ground, high into the sky, and heard him singing his loud, sweet song. She found a picture, copied it, and then signed her name in the space for that day.

'A flower and a bird already,' said Miss Wills. 'How gay our chart will look when it is finished!'

Harry found a butterfly sleeping in the loft. It was a lovely yellow. 'It is a brimstone,' said Miss Wills. 'Well done, Harry. You can make it a fine bright yellow on the chart. Sign your name—that's right.'

'Betty hasn't put anything on the chart yet,' said Pat. 'She said she was going to find heaps of things. But she never does. Where are your eyes, Betty? You never seem to see *any*thing!'

'Oh dear!' said Betty. 'I really will look hard.' So she did. And, on the way to school that morning, as she went down the long lane, she did see something! She was looking in the hedges for an old nest—and she found a new one!

It was a blackbird's nest, and the blackbird was still making it. It was almost finished, and the blackbird was putting a soft lining of grass on to the mud he had placed at the bottom of his nest.

'Oh—he's actually *mak*ing it!' cried Betty,

and she peeped at it to make sure it really was a new one. There it was, set firmly in the fork of a little tree. The tree grew higher than the hedge, and was covered with long catkins that shook in the breeze. The wind blew, and yellow pollen-powder flew from the catkins all over Betty's head.

'I shall have my name on the chart! I shall draw the nest!' cried Betty. She rushed off to school and told Miss Wills.

'I must go and see if it really *is* a blackbird's nest,' said Miss Wills. 'If it is a new one, we mustn't disturb the bird too much or it will fly away and not lay its eggs there.'

Miss Wills, Betty and Jack all went to see if the nest was really a blackbird's. And will you believe it, Betty couldn't find the nest! They hunted up the hedge and down the hedge, but they couldn't find the nest.

'It was well hidden,' said Betty. 'Oh, Miss Wills, can't I count it? Can't I put it on the chart?'

'I'm afraid I must see it,' said Miss Wills. 'Now we really must go back, Betty. It's late.'

Betty was sad. They went back to school, and

on the way there Jack kept looking at Betty's dark hair. He wondered what the yellow powder was, scattered all over it.

And he suddenly knew. 'Of course! It's from the lambs' tail catkins growing in the hedge! Betty must have leaned over to look at the nest, and the hazel tree shook its pollen-powder all over her. Now—if I can find a hazel tree with catkins in the lane, all I have to do is to look in the lower branches for the nest!'

On the way home Jack looked for a hazel tree with catkins. There were two or three growing out of the hedge beside the lane. He looked carefully into the hedge below the trees for a nest.

And he found the blackbird's nest under one of the trees! Above his head the wind shook the lambs' tails, and yellow pollen-powder blew all over Jack's head, just as it had blown over Betty's.

That afternoon Jack took Miss Wills to the nest. 'How did you know where to look for it this time?' asked Miss Wills. Jack told her.

'The nut tree told me. The yellow pollen from the hazel tree's catkins was all over Betty's hair

—so I knew she must have found a nest just below a hazel!'

'Clever boy,' said Miss Wills. 'I think you will have to count the nest as yours, but Betty can sign her name in the space too. A little share of it must be hers, as she first found the nest.'

Betty was sad when she heard that she could not count the nest as hers. 'I am silly not to have noticed where it was,' she said. 'I do think you are clever, Jack, to have seen the yellow stuff on my hair. I wonder why the hazel tree sends out such a lot of powder.'

She went to have a look at the hazel tree on the way home. 'How queer that you should make such a lot of pollen-powder in your long catkins!' she said to the tree. The wind blew and the catkins shook and danced like long tails. Clouds of yellow powder flew out.

'What a waste!' said Betty. 'I wonder why you make that yellow pollen-powder? Is it to help make nuts for us, I wonder?'

The little girl began to look carefully at the bare brown hazel twigs. She saw some tiny buds growing on them—and then, much to her surprise, she saw that some of the buds had tiny red spikes hanging out of the middle of them.

'That's queer!' said Betty to herself. 'That's very queer! Why do some of these little buds have red spikes? Are they a kind of flower-bud?'

She picked two or three twigs with buds on. She took them to school with her, and showed them to Miss Wills.

'Look, Miss Wills,' she said. 'I went to have a peep at the blackbird's nest under the boughs of the hazel tree, and I noticed that some of the hazel buds have these funny red spikes hanging out. What are they?'

'Dear me, Betty *has* begun to use her eyes well!' said Miss Wills, pleased. 'Betty, the hazel tree grows two kinds of flowers—the pollen flowers, which are the lambs' tails we love so much—and these funny little red-spike flowers.'

'What are they for?' asked Betty.

'They make the nuts that we like to pick in the autumn,' said Miss Wills. 'As soon as some of the yellow pollen-powder flies to these red spikes, they can begin to make nuts. I *am* glad you saw them, Betty.'

'Can I draw the catkins and the red-spike

buds on the chart, and sign my name there?'
asked Betty.

'Of course!' said Miss Wills. 'It is one of the
best things we shall have down for this month,
Betty. Well done!'

Betty was very proud. She drew the catkins
on the chart, and she drew and coloured some
of the little buds that had red spikes. She drew
a few that hadn't too.

'They are leaf-buds,' said Miss Wills. 'You
have three things there, Betty, haven't you—the
pollen-catkins—the nut-flowers—and the leaf-
buds? That is really very good.'

'I shall watch the nut-buds and see how the
nuts grow,' said Betty. 'Isn't it funny, Miss
Wills? The blackbird's nest made me see something else! It's fun to find something all by
myself.'

Betty is watching the nut-buds of the hazel
tree. Can *you* find the catkins and the red-spike
buds, and watch the nuts growing too?

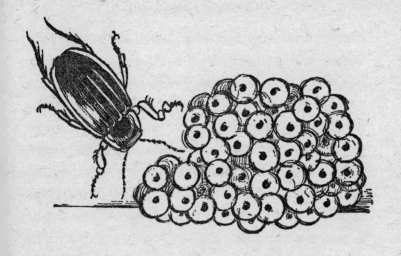

The cross little tadpole

Once upon a time a big mass of jelly lay on the top of a pond. In it were tiny black specks, like little black commas.

The sun shone down and warmed the jelly. A fish tried to nibble a bit, but it was too slippery. A big black beetle tried a little too, but he didn't like it. The rain came and pattered down on the jelly.

Every day the tiny black specks grew bigger. They were eggs. Soon it would be time for them to hatch, and swim about as tadpoles.

The day came when the black eggs had become wriggling tadpoles, and then the jelly began to disappear. It was no longer needed. It had saved the eggs from being eaten, because it was too slippery for any creature to gobble up for its dinner. It had helped to hold the eggs up to the sunshine too. But now it was of no more use.

The little black wrigglers swam to a water-weed and held on to it. They were very tiny. When they were hungry they nibbled the weed. It tasted nice to them.

They grew bigger each day in the pond, and soon the other creatures began to know them. 'There go two tadpoles!' said the stickleback, all his spines standing up along his back.

'Funny creatures, aren't they?' said the big black beetle. 'All head and tail—nothing much else to them!'

'Hundreds of them!' said the water-snail. 'The whole pond is full of them.'

'I like them for my dinner,' said the dragon-fly grub. 'Look—I hide down here in the mud, and when I see a nice fat tadpole swimming by, out I pounce and catch one in my jaw.'

A good many of the tadpoles were eaten by enemies, because they were not sharp enough or fast enough to escape. Those that were left grew big, and raced about the pond, wriggling their long tails swiftly.

One little tadpole had some narrow escapes. One of the black beetles nearly caught him—in fact, a tiny piece was bitten off his tail. Another time he scraped himself badly on the spines of the stickleback.

And twice the dragonfly grub darted at him and almost caught him. Each time the little tadpole was very cross.

'Leave me alone! What harm am I doing to you? I don't want to be your dinner!'

The pond had other things in it besides the fish, the grubs, and the beetles. It had some frogs, and the little tadpole was always in a temper about these.

'Those big fat frogs are so rude and bad-mannered,' he said to the other tadpoles. 'How I hate them with their gaping mouths and great big eyes!'

The frogs didn't like the cross little tadpole because he called rude names after them. Sometimes they chased him, swimming fast with their strong hind legs.

'If once we catch you, we shall spank you hard!' They croaked. The tadpole swam behind a stone and called back to them:

48

'Old croakers! Old greedy-mouths! Old stick-out eyes!'

The frogs tried to overturn the stone and get at the rude tadpole. But he burrowed down in the mud, and came up far behind them.

'Old croakers!' he cried. 'Here I am—peep-bo! Old croakers!'

The frogs lay in wait for the rude tadpole. He never knew when a fat green frog would jump into the water from the bank, almost on top of him. He never knew when one would scramble out of the mud just below him.

'I'm tired of these frogs,' he told the other tadpoles. 'I wish somebody would eat them. I wish those ducks would come back and gobble them up!'

The tadpole had never forgotten one day when some wild ducks had flown down to the pond, and had frightened all the frogs and other creatures very much indeed.

The ducks had caught and eaten three frogs, and at least twenty tadpoles. It had been a dreadful day. None of the tadpoles ever forgot it.

'You shouldn't wish for those ducks to come

back!' said the stickleback. '*You* might be eaten yourself!'

'I'm getting too big to be eaten,' said the tadpole. 'Stickleback, what else eats frogs?'

'The grass-snake eats frogs,' said the pretty little stickleback. 'I once saw him come sliding down into the water. He swam beautifully. He ate four frogs when he came.'

'I've a good mind to go and tell him to come to this pond and eat some more frogs,' said the tadpole. 'He might be glad to know there was a good meal here for him.'

'Well, he is lying in the sun on the bank of the pond, over there,' said the stickleback. 'Go and tell him now! But, tadpole—listen to me—I don't think I have ever met anyone quite so silly as you in all my life!'

'Pooh!' said the tadpole rudely, and swam off towards the bank on which the long grass-snake was lying, curled up in a heap.

The tadpole poked his black head out of the water and called to the snake: 'Hi, grass-snake! Can you hear me?'

The snake woke up in surprise. He looked at the tadpole. 'What do you want?' he said.

'I've come to tell you that there are a lot of horrid, nasty frogs in this pond, that would make a very good dinner for you,' said the tadpole. 'If you slide into the water now I'll show you where to look for them. I'd be glad if you would eat every frog you can see, because they lie in wait for me and try to catch me and spank me.'

The snake put out his quivering tongue and then drew it in again. 'I would come today, but I have just had a very good meal,' he said. 'I will come back some day when I am hungry, and you shall show me where to find the frogs then.'

He glided off through the grass. The tadpole swam back to his friends in excitement.

'What do you think?' he cried. 'I've told the grass-snake about those horrid frogs that want to spank me! He is coming back to eat them one day soon!'

The days went on, warm, sunny days. The tadpole grew and grew. One day he noticed that he had two back legs, and he was most astonished.

'Hallo!' he said. 'I've got legs! So have all the

other tadpoles. I think they are rather nice!'

Then he noticed that he had front legs as well. His tail became shorter. He wanted to breathe up in the air, instead of breathing down in the water.

He and the other tadpoles found a little bit of wood on the surface of the water, and they climbed up on to it. It was nice to sit there in the sunshine, breathing the warm air. It was fun to flick out a little tongue to see if any fly could be caught by it.

'This is a nice life!' said the cross tadpole. 'A very nice life. I like living in this warm pond. Most of those horrid frogs have gone now, so life is very pleasant.'

'There's your friend, the grass-snake,' said the stickleback, poking his head up suddenly. 'Why don't you go and tell him to come and gobble up all the frogs in this pond, as you said you would?'

The tadpole was just about to leap off his bit of wood, when he caught sight of himself in the water. The pond was calm that day, like a mirror, and the tadpole could see himself well.

He stared down at himself in horror and

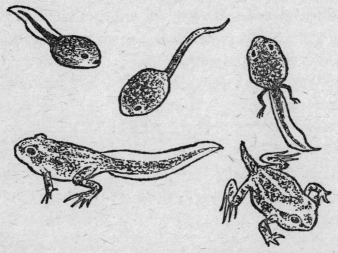

amazement for he did not see a tadpole, but a small frog!

'I've turned into a frog!' he croaked. 'I have, I have! And all the other tadpoles are little frogs too! Why didn't I notice that before?'

'Tadpoles always turn into frogs. I could have told you that before, but you never would listen to anyone,' said the stickleback. 'Well—are you going to find the grass-snake and tell him to come and eat you and all your friends too? You said you would tell him where the frogs were in this pond.'

But the tiny frog did not go to tell the snake anything. He felt quite certain that he would be eaten at once. He jumped into the pond with a splash, and swam as fast as he could to the other side of the water.

Wasn't he a silly fellow? He is five years old now, and quite grown-up—but you have only to say 'Snake!' to him to send him leaping away in fright!

The dandelion clocks

Once there was a dandelion plant. It grew in a very sheltered corner, where the sun was hot, and the wind hardly ever came. It had a rosette of dark-green leaves.

'Why do you grow your leaves like that, in a round bunch?' said the grass near by. 'You keep off all the blades of grass that try to grow near you.'

'Well, that is why I grow my leaves in a round

rosette!' said the dandelion. 'To keep you from growing too close, and taking away light and air from me, and to keep away any other plants!'

'The daisy does that as well,' said a butterfly. 'She grows her leaves in a tight rosette, and won't let anyone else take her little bit of ground. It's a good idea, really.'

'I have a fine big root, as well as a rosette of leaves,' said the dandelion. 'It is a much bigger root than any flower has, in this little corner. It goes right down into the ground.'

'I suppose it holds you tightly in your place,' said the butterfly. 'Well, well—all I can say is that I am very glad *I* haven't a deep root like you, dandelion. I should hate to be tied down in one place. I like to fly about the world, and see all there is to see.'

The dandelion sent up some nice green buds. The butterfly came back again one day to see what sort of flowers the dandelion would have.

'Oh! You are really beautiful!' said the butterfly. 'Yes, you really are. I love your bright yellow head, dandelion—it is prettier even than the daisy's head.'

The dandelion flowers shone brightly on their

green stalks. They were very bright in the sun.

'Aren't you afraid of some animal coming along and eating you?' asked the butterfly. 'You are so bright, with your yellow heads of flowers, that I am sure a cow or horse would see you at once, and nibble you to bits!'

'I taste nasty,' said the dandelion. 'I have a milky juice in my stalks that tastes bitter. No animal will go on nibbling me, once it has tasted my nasty juice.'

'It seems to me that you are rather a clever plant,' said the butterfly. 'With your leaf-rosette, your long, deep root, and your nasty milky juice! I shall come back again and see you another day. Perhaps you will have another clever idea to tell me.'

She flew off, and the dandelion opened

another golden bud in the sun. Soon the whole plant was yellow with brilliant golden blossoms, and was beautiful in the summer sunshine. Nobody ate it. Nobody harmed it. It flowered in peace and safety.

One by one the yellow flowers faded and died. Soon there was not one left. When the butterfly came back one day, it was surprised to see the plant without its golden blossoms.

'You are growing old, dandelion,' said the butterfly. 'I can see your golden hairs turning to grey, and you are hiding your head!'

All the flower-stalks had drooped, and all the golden heads were, as the butterfly said, turning grey. They lay among the grass, looking faded and sad.

'Yes, your hair is going grey,' said the butterfly, looking at the old flower-heads. 'What a pity! Can't you raise your heads up any more? Do you feel so tired and old?'

'No,' said the dandelion. 'I don't feel at all tired. All I am doing is resting my flower-heads whilst they make seed for me.'

'Seed!' said the butterfly, 'What is seed?'

'Ah, seed is the most important thing of all to

a plant,' said the dandelion. 'Without seed we cannot go on and on growing new plants each year. I want to send out my seeds so that I may know that there will be hundreds of new little dandelion plants growing everywhere!'

'Oh,' said the butterfly. 'I know how you feel about it, dandelion. It is the same as I feel about eggs. I want to lay many eggs, so that they will hatch into caterpillars that will grow into butterflies like me. You want children like yourself, and I want children like *my*self. That is a rule of life, isn't it?'

'I don't know what a rule of life is,' said the dandelion. 'All I know is that I must make seed, and send it out into the world to grow.'

'And I must lay eggs,' said the butterfly. 'I know where I shall lay my eggs too. I am a cabbage butterfly and I shall lay my eggs on the underside of a cabbage leaf, so that when they hatch out, there will be plenty of good food for my caterpillars to feed on.'

The dandelion was not listening. She was slowly lifting up one of her flower-stalks. She raised it high—and higher—and the butterfly stared in surprise.

'Dandelion! Did you know that your flower-stalk had grown very, very long whilst it has lain in the grass? It is so tall that now you will be able to see much farther!'

'I haven't eyes like you,' said the dandelion, beginning to lift another stalk. 'Yes—I know that my stalks have grown tall. There is a reason for that.'

'Is there?' said the butterfly. 'Do tell me.'

'Well,' said the dandelion, 'look at my old flower-heads, on the top of their long stalks. As you said, they have turned grey—but the grey is the plumes that belong to my seeds. Look carefully, and you will see what I mean.'

The butterfly flew down close beside a grey-plumed head, and looked at it carefully.

'Dandelion,' she said, 'your old flower-heads have all grown tiny seeds, each with its own parachute of silky hairs. How wonderful! I have never seen such a marvellous change in my life. You are the cleverest plant I know.'

'There are many cleverer than I am,' said the dandelion. 'We all have our own tricks and ways, butterfly. Now you see why I have grown my stalks so long—I want to take my seeds high up into the air, where the sun can warm them, and the wind can blow them.'

'Why do you want the wind to blow them?' said the butterfly in surprise.

'I want the wind to take each of my seeds far away from me,' said the dandelion. 'As far away as it can! I do not want dozens of tiny dandelions growing near me, all choking one another. I want the wind to blow them far away.'

'And so you have given each seed a parachute of silky hairs to carry it away!' said the butterfly. 'Well, what a marvellous idea, to be sure. May I blow one?'

'Your breath won't move a seed!' said the dandelion.

The butterfly blew—but the dandelion was right. Not one seed moved away from the stalk-head. The seeds stood on a kind of cushion, and they made a most beautiful globe of grey-white.

One by one the stalks raised themselves up into the air, and soon there were about twelve lovely dandelion 'clocks' standing in the little sheltered corner. The butterfly thought she had never seen anything so beautiful.

The dandelion clocks

'When will the wind come and blow your seeds away for you?' she asked. 'I want to see them fly in the air.'

'Soon, I hope,' said the dandelion, and the plant and the butterfly waited patiently for the wind to come.

But it didn't come. The corner that the dandelion grew in was very, very sheltered. Hardly any wind ever came to it. The tall clocks stood there, not moving. No seed blew away at all.

The dandelion grew anxious. 'Oh, I do hope the wind comes soon!' it said. 'I don't want seeds to fall off to the ground. They must not grow too near to me. Oh, how I wish the wind would come!'

After a while, there came the sound of children's voices, and a boy and two girls came into the sheltered corner. They stopped in delight.

'Harry! Look! What lovely dandelion clocks!' cried a girl's voice. 'Let's pick them and blow them to tell the time!'

Then, in a trice, all the dandelion clocks were picked, and the children danced away with them. They blew hard at the clocks. 'Puff! One o'clock. Puff! Two o'clock. Puff! Three o'clock.'

The seeds flew off, each with their tiny parachute of hairs. They flew far away, and then fell gently to the ground. The butterfly flew round the children's heads and watched the seeds flying away.

She flew back to the dandelion plant. 'Your seeds have all gone to their new homes,' she said. 'There will be hundreds of tiny new dandelions next year, so you can be happy. The

children made little winds with their mouths and blew the seeds away!'

'Good,' said the dandelion. 'Now I am happy, and I can take a rest. Go and lay your eggs, butterfly, and be happy too!'

The very queer chicks

Once there was a hen who wanted to sit on eggs.
The farmer's wife was pleased.

'Here is a hen who wants to sit on eggs every
day and night!' she said. 'We will give her some
duck's eggs to sit on. The duck is a bad mother.
She will not sit long enough on her eggs!'

So the farmer's wife took twelve duck's eggs,
and put them in a nest of straw. She set the old
brown hen on the greeny-blue eggs, and the big
bird settled down at once. She was happy.

'This is what I wanted!' she said to her friend,
the white hen. 'I wanted to feel a lot of eggs

under me. I wanted to cover them, and keep them warm. I am happy now.'

Her friend was sitting on eggs too, but they were hen's eggs, not duck's. Both the birds were happy. They loved sitting on the big clutches of eggs.

They sat on them for many days. Sometimes they left them for a little while to pick up some grain, or to have a drink of water. But they soon went back, fluffed themselves out well, and covered the eggs with their feathers and moist warm bodies.

'We must not let them get cold or too dry,' said the white hen.

'If we do, they will not hatch out into little chicks,' said the brown hen. 'Cluck-cluck. We will keep them very warm.'

One day the white hen was excited. She bent her head down and listened.

'What is the matter?' said the brown hen.

'My eggs are going to hatch!' said the white hen. 'I can hear one little chick tapping with his beak inside the egg. Soon it will break—and I shall see a dear little fluffy chick!'

The white hen was right. Before the next

morning, all her eggs were hatched. She had twelve little chicks. Six of them were bright yellow, and six of them were a mixture of brown and yellow. They ran about, and cheeped in little high voices. It was sweet to hear them.

Then the eggs of the brown hen hatched too. Out came, not chicks, but twelve little ducklings. They were all bright yellow. The hen was very pleased with them. She thought they were chicks and she clucked to them lovingly.

'Dear little chicks of mine! I will take care of you! When you hear me call sharply, like this—CLUCK-CLUCK—you must run to me at once, and hide under my wings.

The chicks and the ducklings knew their own mother hens. The chicks always ran to the white hen when she called them, and the ducklings always ran to the brown hen.

Sometimes the cat came into the farmyard, and the hens would cluck loudly. 'An enemy is near! CLUCK-CLUCK! Come here, come here, an enemy is near!'

Then the little chicks would run to the white hen and hide under her feathers, and the little ducklings would run to the brown hen.

It was funny to see their heads peeping out from the feathers of the hens. First one little head would pop out and then another and another, until it seemed as if each hen had one big head and many little ones!

The hens tried to teach their little ones all the things they should know. 'This is the way to scratch in the ground, to see if any grain of corn is buried there,' the white hen would say to her chicks. And she would scratch hard at the earth with her short, strong legs, and big, blunt claws.

Then she would peck up a grain of corn with her strong beak. She was very good at scratching with her feet, and pecking with her beak.

Sometimes, when a chick was naughty, she would give him a sharp peck. Then he would be good again for quite a long while.

It was a happy time in the farmyard for the little chicks and ducks. The sun was warm. There were many things to see and hear. There was the old sow, grunting in her sty. There were the great big cows that came to the milking-shed. There were the white ducks that waddled to the round pond.

The ducklings grew fast, and so did the chicks. They ran with one another, and cheeped in their high voices. It was fun in the farmyard, and there were always their mothers to run to if they were afraid of anything.

One day the ducklings saw the pond. One duckling had gone after the ducks, when they had waddled to the pond, and he had suddenly seen the big stretch of water.

'What is it? What is it?' he cheeped. He ran to the other chicks and ducklings, and made them come with him to see this wonderful thing.

'Pooh!' said the chicks. 'What a thing to bring us here to see! Just water!'

'Is that what it is? Water!' said the ducklings, who were most excited to see the pond.

'Yes,' said the biggest chick. 'You had better come away from it. Our mothers say it is not good for us.'

'But it looks lovely! It looks very, very good! We love it!' said all the little yellow ducklings, and one of them took a step nearer.

The brown hen saw him. 'CLUCK-CLUCK-CLUCK!' she cried. 'Bad little chick! Come here at once. How dare you go near that pond!

She ran at the ducklings, and chased them away from the water. But they did not forget it. They kept thinking of it, and talking about it.

One morning it rained so hard that a big puddle was made in the farmyard. The ducklings found it and waddled into it joyfully. Oh, how lovely it felt!

The brown hen saw them, and she was very angry indeed. 'How dare you get your feet wet?' she said. 'You bad little chicks! How dare you get wet? Don't you know that chicks never get wet if they can help it?'

But the ducklings loved the puddle, and they were very sorry when it dried up.

'Let's go and find that pond again,' said the biggest duckling. 'I want to get my feet wet. I want to get right into the water. I want to paddle in it.'

All the ducklings felt the same. The chicks would not come with them. 'What! Go into that horrid wet, cold water! Get our feet wet and our feathers damp?' they cheeped. 'Of course not!'

So the ducklings went alone. They came to the pond. They stood by the edge. They put their little feet into the water, and it felt lovely.

The brown hen came rushing up. 'Come away at once, at once, at once! Come away! CLUCK-CLUCK-CLUCK!'

But this time the ducklings did not listen to her. One duckling jumped straight into the pond—splash! And then another and another went in—splash, splash, splash! They were all in, and swimming beautifully, their little webbed feet paddling along, pushing themselves forward! It was sweet to see them.

The old mother hen was afraid for them. She

ran up and down the bank of the pond, squawking so loudly that the farmer's wife came out to see what was the matter.

'Oh!' she said. 'Poor old mother hen—your babies have gone into the pond. But don't worry—they are not chicks, but ducklings!'

'Cluck, cluck!' said the hen, in great surprise. She had always thought they were chicks.

'They are made for swimming in the water,' said the farmer's wife. She called one of her big white ducks to her. 'See,' she said to the anxious hen, 'the duck's feet are made for swimming— they have webbed skin between the toes. Yours are not webbed, but they are strong to help you to scratch for grain. You have strong claws too, to help you.'

'Cluck-cluck!' said the hen, beginning to understand.

'Look at the duck's beak,' said the farmer's wife. 'It is quite different from yours, henny-penny! It is flat and hollow; and do you see these holes? They let out the water and the mud when the duck dives into the mud to hunt for water-insects. The insects are left behind in the duck's beak, and she eats them—but the water and the mud drain out!'

'Cluck-cluck!' said the hen.

'Chicks will be hens and ducklings will be ducks,' said the farmer's wife, letting the duck waddle away. 'Ducks will always waddle because their legs are put so far back to help them to swim well. Hens will always run and scratch.'

73

'Cluck-cluck!' said the hen, listening.

'Hens will always peck up their grain, and ducks will always shovel their beaks in the mud,' said the farmer's wife. 'That is why you have such different beaks. Don't scold your babies, henny-penny. It is I you should scold, for it was I who gave you duck's eggs to sit on, instead of hen's eggs!'

'Cluck-cluck!' said the hen, and stared at her little babies swimming on the pond. She didn't scold them when they came out. She looked at their spoon-shaped beaks, and at their webbed feet, and knew that they were ducklings.

'What a mistake I made!' she said. 'I brought them up to be good chicks—but they will all grow into ducks!'

The swallows in the barn

One fine day in the early summer, two dark-blue swallows flew into the farmer's old barn. They perched up in the roof, and talked to one another.

'We will build our nest here, on this big wooden beam. This is just the place!'

They flew out again and went to the farmer's pond, where the white ducks swam. They flew down to the muddy edge, and took up a little of the mud in their beaks.

'Why do you want mud?' quacked the ducks in astonishment.

'We make our nests of mud!' twittered the swallows. 'We mix the mud with a little hair, or a little straw from the yard. Then it makes a very fine nest.'

'We shall line it with grass and a few soft feathers,' said the mother swallow. 'Then I shall lay my eggs there. Good-bye! We will come and fetch some more mud soon.'

The swallows made their mud-nest on the big wooden beam. Then they lined it softly. The mother swallow sat in it and laid four white eggs, speckled with brown and grey. She was very proud of them.

'We shall soon have some baby birds of our own,' she said to her mate. 'I will sit on the eggs to keep them warm. Go and fly in the air, and catch me a beakful of insects. I shall soon be hungry.'

Her little mate fed her well whilst she sat on the eggs and kept them warm. One day the swallow was excited.

'Our eggs are hatching!' she twittered. 'Listen! The shells are breaking!'

Four tiny birds came out of the eggs. The swallows were full of joy. But how busy they were each day now, for they had four babies to feed as well as themselves!

They flew high in the air on their strong wings, all day long, opening their wide beaks and catching hundreds of flies for their little ones. Many other swallows were doing the same thing. The air seemed full of flashing wings and long forked tails, as the swallows darted here and there in the blue summer sky.

Outside the barn, just under the eaves, was another nest. It belonged to a pair of noisy, untidy sparrows. They too had laid eggs which had hatched. But their babies were already big, and were almost ready to fly.

'Chirrup, chirrup!' said the sparrows, all day long.

'Twitter, twitter, twitter!' said the swallows, in their sweet, high voices.

Sometimes the sparrows flew into the barn to see how the baby swallows were getting on. Sometimes the swallows went to see the baby sparrows. It was fun to have two little families growing up together.

One day a big rat came into the barn. He ran up the big beams in the wall of the barn. He came to the beam where the swallows' nest lay. He was hungry. He wanted baby birds to eat.

The two swallows were out in the sky, hunting for insects. Only the four tiny swallows were in the nest. But into the barn flew the mother sparrow, and she saw the big grey rat.

'Chirrup, chirrup!' she called, and flew round the rat in anger. 'Go away! I will call the stable cat in here! Go away!'

The cock-sparrow flew in when he heard his mate chirrup in anger. 'Fetch the cat, fetch the cat!' cried the hen-sparrow.

The cock-sparrow flew out. The cat was sitting in the sunshine outside. The sparrow flew round her head, and she jumped up. She wanted to catch the sparrow for her dinner. But he flew off in front of her.

The cat ran after him on her soft paws. He flew into the barn again, and the cat darted in too.

'Here comes the cat, here comes the cat!' called the mother sparrow in delight. The rat was afraid. He turned away from the swallows' nest, and ran along another beam, hoping that the cat would not see him.

She smelt him, and then she saw him. She darted up a beam and chased him. He fled away down a hole, making up his mind that he would not go into the barn again! The cat went out into the sunshine.

How glad the two swallows were when they knew that their little ones were safe! 'Thank you, thank you!' they twittered again and again to the sparrows. 'You saved our little ones from the rat. We will always be friends with you. Our children shall be friends too.'

So, when the young sparrows and young swallows had all learnt to fly, they became friends. The little blue swallows did not like perching in trees with the little brown sparrows, and the sparrows did not like flying too high in the air. But they often flew round the trees together, and chirruped and twittered merrily.

Summer went. Autumn came. The young sparrows had learnt a great deal, for they were always talking together with other birds. They spoke to their swallow friends about the winter days.

'Soon it will be cold weather. But we shall have fun then. We will take you to the farmyard and show you where to find spilt corn. We will take you to the hedges and show you good seeds. We will play games together, and make as much noise as we like.'

'We shan't be here then,' said the young swallows. 'You see, we don't eat seeds. Our beaks are not strong enough. We eat insects. We shall fly away when the cold days come, and leave you.'

'Oh no! Don't do that!' cried the sparrows. 'We should miss you dreadfully. Stay here. We will ask the robin to catch insects for you.'

'He won't do that,' said the swallows. 'He will hardly find enough for himself. He has told us that there are hardly any in the winter. We cannot starve, so we will have to fly away from here.'

'Where will you go to?' asked the sparrows, very sadly.

'A long way away,' said the swallows. 'We shall fly to a warm country, where the sun will still be hot, and where there will be plenty of insects for us to eat.'

'How will you know the way?' asked the sparrows. 'You have never been there before.'

'We shall find the way all right,' said the swallows. 'The wind will help us too. It will blow behind us. We shall miss you, dear little friends.'

'Please don't go. Do stay,' begged the young sparrows. 'Surely just four swallows can find enough food for the winter.'

'Well—we will see,' said the little swallows. 'We don't want to leave this farm-yard that we love, or the pond we skim over, or the barn we know so well. Maybe we will stay after all.'

But one day in the autumn the young swallows felt very restless. A cold wind had begun to blow. There did not seem to be so many insects. They flew here and there on their wide, strong wings, and suddenly they did not want to stay near the farm-yard any more.

One swallow after another settled on the roof of the old barn. Dozens of them, scores of them, hundreds of them gathered together, twittering.

'It is time to go. Say good-bye! It is time to go! We will fly tonight, tonight!'

The young swallows said good-bye to the sparrows. 'We must go after all. We cannot stay.

The wind is blowing to help us. We shall never forget you.'

'Come back again,' begged the sparrows. 'You were born here, in the old barn. You grew up in the sky above the fields and the farm. Your home is really here. Come back again. We shall look out for you!'

'We will come back,' promised the young swallows. 'Good-bye! We must go, we must go!'

And that evening they flew away in a great flock of many hundreds. Their steel-blue wings beat the air, and their voices twittered high.

'We are going! Good-bye! But we will come back again.'

Now they are gone and the little sparrows are lonely without their friends. But one day in April, when the sun is warm and the sky is blue, the swallows will come back.

Yes—the little swallows born in the old barn, will come back to the farm-yard, back to the barn, and will build their nest there for their own little young ones. Wait patiently, little brown sparrows—find seeds for your winter food—fly round the farm-yard you know so well.

And then one day you will see the swallows again, back from their winter home. Chirrup, chirrup, twitter, twitter! What joy to be all together again once more!

The dog who wanted a home

There was once a dog who wanted a home. He had had a bad master, who whipped him every day, and he had run away because he was so unhappy.

'I shall find a new master, or perhaps a mistress,' said the dog to himself. 'I want someone who will love me. I want someone to love and to care for.'

But nobody seemed to want a dog, nobody at all. It was very sad. The dog ran here and he ran there, but either there was already a dog in the houses he went to, or the people there didn't want a dog.

He talked to his friend, the cat, about it. 'What am I to do?' he said. 'I must have a home. I cannot run about wild, with no food, and only the puddles to drink from.'

'Dogs and cats need homes,' said the cat, licking herself as she sat on top of the wall. 'I don't know of anyone who wants a dog. It's a pity you are not a cat.'

'Why?' asked the dog.

'Because I know a poor, blind old lady who badly wants a cat,' said the cat. 'She is lonely, and she wants a nice, cosy cat she can have in her lap.'

'Perhaps she would have a dog instead,' said the dog. 'If she is blind, I could help her, couldn't I? I could take her safely across the roads, and guard her house at night. A cat couldn't do that.'

'Well, she says she wants a cat, not a dog,' said the cat. Then she stopped licking herself and looked closely at the dog.

'I have an idea!' she said. 'You have a very silky coat for a dog, and a very long tail. I wonder whether you could pretend to be a cat! The poor old lady is blind, she wouldn't know.'

'I shouldn't like to deceive anyone,' said the dog.

'No, that wouldn't be nice,' said the cat. 'But after all, a dog *would* be better for the old lady, and when she got used to you, you could tell her you were a dog, and ask her to forgive you for pretending.'

'And by that time she might be so fond of me that she wouldn't mind keeping me!' said the dog joyfully. 'Yes—that is quite a good idea of yours, cat.'

'I will give you a few hints about cats,' said the cat. 'Don't bark, whatever you do, because, as you know, cats mew. If you bark you will give yourself away. And do try and purr a little.'

The dog tried—but what came from his throat was more of a growl than a purr. The cat laughed.

'That's really enough to make a cat laugh!' she said. 'Well, perhaps with a little practice you may get better. And another thing to remember is—put your claws in when you walk, so that you walk softly, like me, and don't make a clattering sound.'

The dog looked at his paws. The big, blunt

claws stuck out, and he could not move them back into his paws, as the cat could. 'I must try to practise that too,' he said.

'Good-bye,' said the cat. 'I wish you luck. She is a dear old lady and will be very kind to you.'

The dog ran off to the old lady's house. She was sitting in her kitchen, knitting. The dog ran up to her, and pressed against her, as he had seen cats do. The old lady put down her hand and stroked him.

'So someone has sent me a cat!' she said. 'How kind! Puss, puss, puss, do you want some milk?'

She got up and put down a saucer of milk. The dog was pleased. He lapped it up noisily.

'Dear me, what a noise you make!' said the old lady in surprise. 'You must be a very hungry cat! Come on to my knee.'

The dog jumped up on to the old lady's knee. She stroked his silky coat, and felt his long tail. He tried his very best to purr. He made a very funny noise.

'You must have got a cold, Puss,' said the old lady. 'That's a funny purr you have! Now, go to sleep.

The dog fell asleep. He liked being in the old lady's warm lap. He felt loved and happy. If only she went on thinking that he was a cat!

When he woke up, the old lady spoke to him. 'Puss, I want you to lie in the kitchen tonight and catch the mice that come. You will be very useful to me if you can do that.'

The dog was not good at catching mice. He was not quiet and sly like the cat. But he made up his mind to try. He did try, very hard, but as soon as he jumped up when he saw a mouse, the little animal heard his claws clattering on the floor, and fled away.

So in the moring there were no dead mice for the old lady to find. She was quite nice about it and stroked the dog gently.

'Never mind, Puss,' she said. 'You can try again tonight.'

The old lady was so kind and gentle that the dog longed with all his heart to catch mice for her, or to do anything to please her. He trotted after her all day long, as she went about her work. It was wonderful what she could do without being able to see.

'The only thing I can't do with safety is to go

out and see my grandchildren,' she told the dog. 'You see, I have to cross two roads to get to their house, and I am always afraid of being knocked over by something I can't see.'

The dog nearly said, 'Woof, woof, I will help you,' and just remembered in time that cats never bark.

The old lady was puzzled that day. Every time the dog ran across the floor she put her head on one side and listened.

'Your paws make such a noise,' she said. 'Surely you put your sharp claws in as you run, Puss? It sounds as if you are making quite a noise with them.'

So the dog was, because he couldn't help it. He couldn't put his claws in, like the cat. No dog can.

Then another thing puzzled the old lady. She put some milk on her finger for the dog to lick. The dog put out his pink tongue and licked the milk away.

'Well!' said the old lady, surprised. 'What a queer tongue you have, Puss! All the other cats I have had had very rough, scraping tongues— but you have a very smooth one!'

'Oh dear!' thought the dog. 'This is quite true. Dogs have smooth tongues, and cats have rough ones. I remember an old cat licking me once, and I noticed how rough her tongue was— almost as if it was covered with tiny hooks!'

'I'll give you a nice meaty bone, Puss,' said the old lady at tea-time. 'You can scrape the meat off it with your tongue, and when you have taken away the meat, we will give the bone to the next-door dog to crunch. Cats cannot crunch bones, but dogs can!'

The dog was delighted to see the lovely, meaty bone. He lay down and began to lick it with his tongue, as cats do. But his tongue was not rough, and he could not get the meat off the bone, any more than you could with *your* tongue!

It was sad. He was hungry and longed to crunch up the bone. He sniffed at it. He licked it again. Then he got it into his mouth and gave it a bite with his hard, strong dog's teeth, that were so different from the teeth of cats!

The bone made a noise as he crunched it up. The old lady was surprised. 'Well, I never heard a cat crunch up a big bone before!' she said. 'You must have strong teeth, Puss!'

She put on her hat and coat. 'I am going out,' she said. 'I shall try to get to the house where my grandchildren live. Maybe someone will help me across the road. Keep house for me whilst I am gone, Puss.'

The dog did not like to see the blind old lady going out alone. He ran after her. When she came to the road she had to cross, he stood in front of her, making her wait until a bicycle had gone by. Then he gently tugged at her dress to show her that it was safe to go across.

The old lady was delighted. She bent down to stroke the dog. 'Puss, you are the cleverest cat in the world!' she said.

But dear me, when the old lady reached her grandchildren safely, what a surprise for her! They ran out to greet her, all shouting the same thing.

'Granny! You've got a dog! Oh, what a nice one!'

And so at last the secret was out. 'No wonder I was so puzzled!' said the old lady, stooping to pat the dog. He barked a little, and licked her hand, wagging his tail hard.

'That's right!' said the old lady. 'Don't

pretend to be a cat any more! Bark, and lick my hand and wag your tail! I'll have you instead of a cat. You're a kind little animal, and you'll help me across the road, won't you?'

'Woof, woof, woof!' said the dog joyfully, and ran off to tell the cat that he had found a home at last.

These are other Knight Books

Enid Blyton
THE FISH THAT BUILT A NEST

The stickleback thought that a nest, like birds
build, was a wonderful way to keep eggs and
and young fish safe. The other pond creatures
thought it a strange idea but the stickleback
was determined. He collected all the weed,
straw and grass he could find and began to
build a nest in the reeds.

Another collection of nine nature stories.

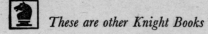
These are other Knight Books

Also published in Knight Books are Enid Blyton's 'Secret Seven' books. Here is a list of the titles:

THE SECRET SEVEN

SECRET SEVEN ADVENTURE

WELL DONE, SECRET SEVEN

SECRET SEVEN ON THE TRAIL

GO AHEAD, SECRET SEVEN

GOOD WORK, SECRET SEVEN

SECRET SEVEN WIN THROUGH

THREE CHEERS, SECRET SEVEN

SECRET SEVEN MYSTERY

PUZZLE FOR THE SECRET SEVEN

SECRET SEVEN FIREWORKS

GOOD OLD SECRET SEVEN

SHOCK FOR THE SECRET SEVEN

LOOK OUT SECRET SEVEN

FUN FOR THE SECRET SEVEN

Ask your bookseller, or at your public library, for details of other Knight Books, or write to Editor-in-Chief, Knight Books Arlen House, Salisbury Road, Leicester, LE1 7QS.